"PROBLEMS AREN'T THE PROBLEM; COPING IS THE PROBLEM."
VIRGINIA SATIR

For my parents, who always knew how to make everything okay.

Special thanks to Mati; it is a joy working with your whimsy and humor.

Copyright 2015 Carole P. Roman All rights reserved.
ISBN: 978-1-48359-226-8
Library of Congress Control Number: 2012921018
CreateSpace Independent Publishing Platform,
North Charleston, SC

ONE TO TEN

SQUIRREL'S BAD DAY

By Carole P. Roman

Illustrated by Mateya Arkova

LA, LA, LA...

OOPS...

Aww...

AH HA...　　　　LA LA LA...　　　　OUCH...

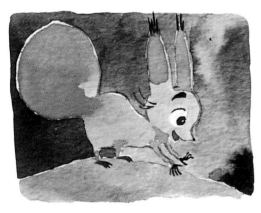

OOMPF...　　　SIGH...　　　WAAAH!

Oh no! That's terrible. I can't believe it! You poor thing.
Don't be sad about the acorns.

I have an idea. My mom taught me a special trick to do when I'm upset. Let's figure out how bad this really is. We can rate it on a special chart.

Forest friends, come and help us out. Let's say that Red Bird is squirrel's best friend. Red Bird is flying away for the winter to be with her family. This news could make Squirrel upset. She will miss her friend. Using a scale with ten being the worst thing ever and one, no problem at all, what number describes how you might feel about it?

12

14

THE RAIN AND WIND CAME RUINING OUR FUN. WE HAD TO STOP PLAYING.

IT WAS A MESS.

LET'S GIVE THE ONE-TO-TEN GAME A TRY. WHAT NUMBER ARE YOU THINK-ING? THERE ARE A LOT OF DIFFERENT NUMBERS. RED BIRD, YOU'RE SAYING IT'S A SEVEN. FROGGY GAVE IT A ONE. HEY, GUYS, DON'T YOU REMEMBER WHAT HAPPENED NEXT?

How about that skating party last winter, Little Fox?

You were showing off your how fast you could skate when you slipped on the ice.
You were so embarrassed.
Where does it fall on our chart of one to ten?

21

You want to say ten, because everyone was laughing. Poor Foxy's face was as red as his bushy tail. You can't give it a ten, my little friend, and eight is stretching it. Shall we settle on seven?

Don't you recall something good coming out of it? You worked hard and became the best skater in our group!

Froggy wants to try Rabbit's ratings list. Froggy is thinking about a number from one to ten. Where shall Froggy put this problem? Froggy thinks eight because Mama was mad. What do you think? Six, you say?

Well, maybe it could be a six. Froggy did do some extra credit, and the teacher sent home a gold star. There is no place to go, but to hop up from there.

I remember when my dear, deer parents made separate homes. That's surely a ten.

This one is hard. Half of you is sad, and the other half is probably relieved there will be less fighting. Feeling like a nine is okay until you get used to your new itff. Ift's consider it an eight, even though your heart says it's a nine.

Your hamster died. He was old and had gotten sick. You brought him to the doctor, and there was nothing they could do to make him better. I think we know what this one has to be. It doesn't get much worse than this. Yep, it's a ten.

Everybody has times they have to use this system.
How about when someone's grandma and grandpa move far away?

Who is going to bake carrot cookies and read me books over and over? Who's going to babysit and tickle the spot between my ears?

So, Squirrel, how do you feel about those acorns now?

35

In the event that something happens,
And you feel your world fly apart,
Recall this conversation;
Remember the one to ten chart.

When you have a problem,
Whether it's big or small,
Think of a number to rate it.
Maybe it won't bother you at all.

One through five is pretty low.
Six through eight are not.
Nine and ten sound kind of bad.
The truth is they don't happen a lot.

Once you give it a number,
(And please be honest about it too)
The problem doesn't feel so big,
And somehow you'll know what to do.